OOGLE-FLIP
and the
Planet Adventure

Written by Andrew Norton
Illustrated by Christy Croll

For Angus, Katrina and Patrick – I should have written this sooner.
A.N.

For E.W.C. and G.C., you are the center of my universe.
C.C.

Oogle-Flip, the brave explorer,

springs aboard his rocket ship.

He is going hunting planets, into space – it's quite a trip!

Oogle wants to find a planet where the Flips might holiday.

He will have a
grand adventure
finding somewhere
new to play.

"You won't find another planet
that's as suitable as here."

"Good luck, though!" his friends all say,
and send him off with rousing cheers.

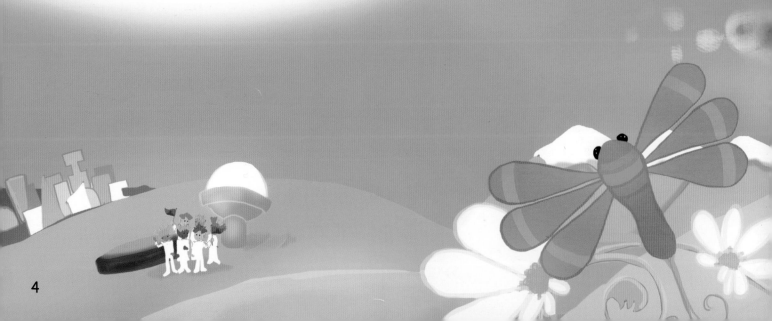

4

Oogle's sure that he will triumph.
"Many stars there are in sight,
Planets orbit most of them
and some for life must be just right."

5

Oogle-Flip's now in his spaceship,
planet-hunting, star to star.
Is there one as fine as Flip-World?
He may have to travel far…

Flip World

outgoin

many plan

6

Stars are balls of burning gases.

Small ones merely glow red-hot.

Big ones burn with white-hot fierceness.

Some have planets, some have not.

Planets may be gas or rocky, circling stars in endless race.

Some stay close to their star, some have orbits far in space.

Here's a planet, rainbow colored, wrapped in stripes of swirling cloud. Oogle-Flip thinks, "Pretty, it looks."

Then he stops and cries aloud:

"Land on such a planet, I can't!"
"Where's the surface?" Oogle pleads.
This one's much too insubstantial.

Solid ground is what he needs.

giant planet made of gas

outgoing message:
no surface there is

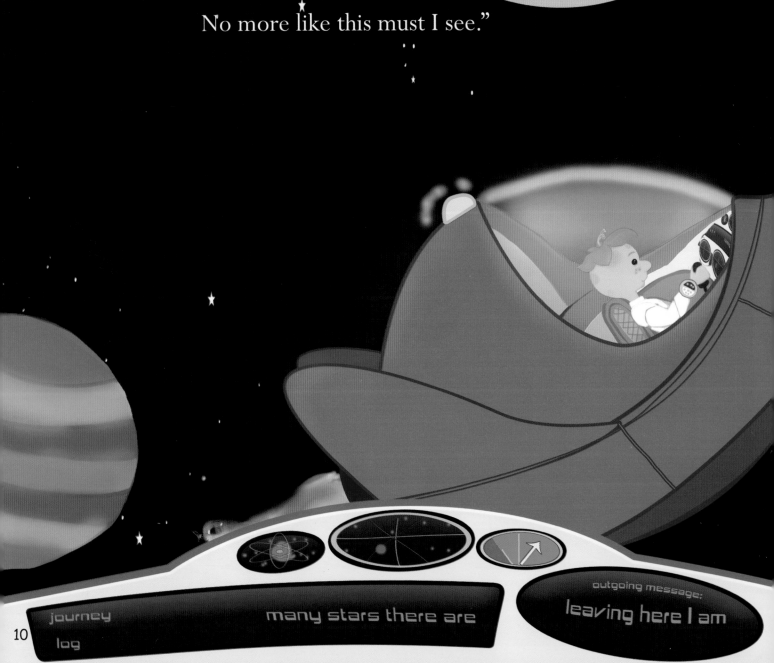

"Giant planets made of gas
are not the type of world for me.
Somewhere with a surface, I need.
No more like this must I see."

journey
log

many stars there are

outgoing message:
leaving here I am

Here's a planet, red and fiery...

..even rocks begin to melt!

Oogle sweats inside his spaceship,
"Never so hot have I felt!"
"Stay near such a planet, I can't!
Boil, I would, and leave no trace!"

This one's much too hot for Oogle.
Time to find a cooler place.

"Planets so close to their stars
are not the type of world for me.
Somewhere farther distant, I need.
No more like this must I see."

Here's a planet dark and grim,
Its distant star provides no heat.
Oogle's hands and toes are frozen,
and he cannot feel his feet.

"Stand on such a planet, I can't!
Freeze I would, and turn to ice."
This one's much too cold for Oogle.
Somewhere warmer would be nice.

"Planets so far from their stars
are not the type of world for me.
One at middle distance, I need.
No more like this must I see."

Here's a planet, large and heavy.

Its gravity is very strong.

Oogle-Flip is squashed and flattened.

"On this world I don't belong!"

"Move on such a planet, I can't!

Even lifting-off is tough."

This one's much too big for Oogle. Can he find one small enough?

"Massive planets made
of rock are not the type
of world for me.
Somewhere smaller
than this, I need.
No more like this must I see."

journey

gravity

too

log

Here's a planet, small and rocky.
Its gravity is very weak.
Oogle wonders where the air's gone.
"Into space it must have leaked."
"Breathe on such a planet, I can't!
Keep my helmet on, I should."

This one's much too small for Oogle.
Yet another proves no good.

"Little planets made of rock
are not the type of world for me.
They can't keep their atmospheres.
No more like this must I see."

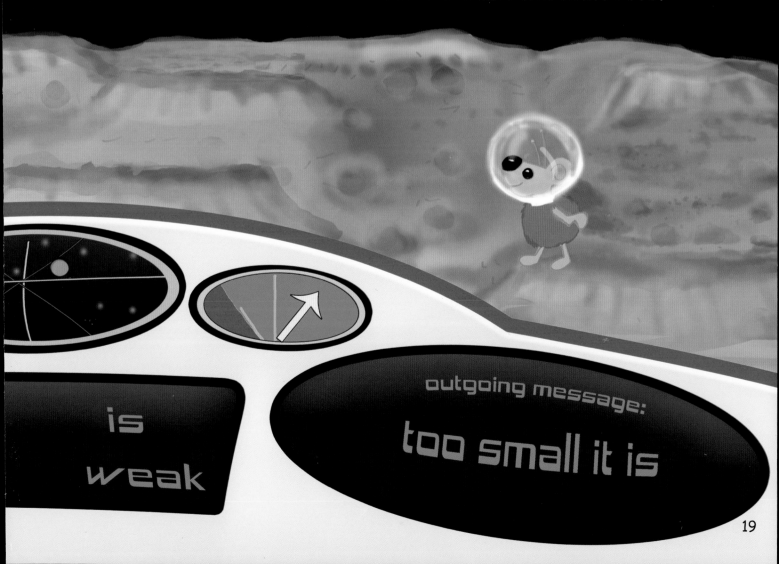

is
weak

outgoing message:
too small it is

Oogle wonders if he'll ever
find a world where he could thrive.
"Somewhere warm and pleasant, I need.
On that planet I'd survive."

"Giant planets made of gas are
pretty, but they have no soil.

Planets too close to their stars are
hot enough to make me boil.

Planets too far from their
stars are cold enough to
make me freeze.

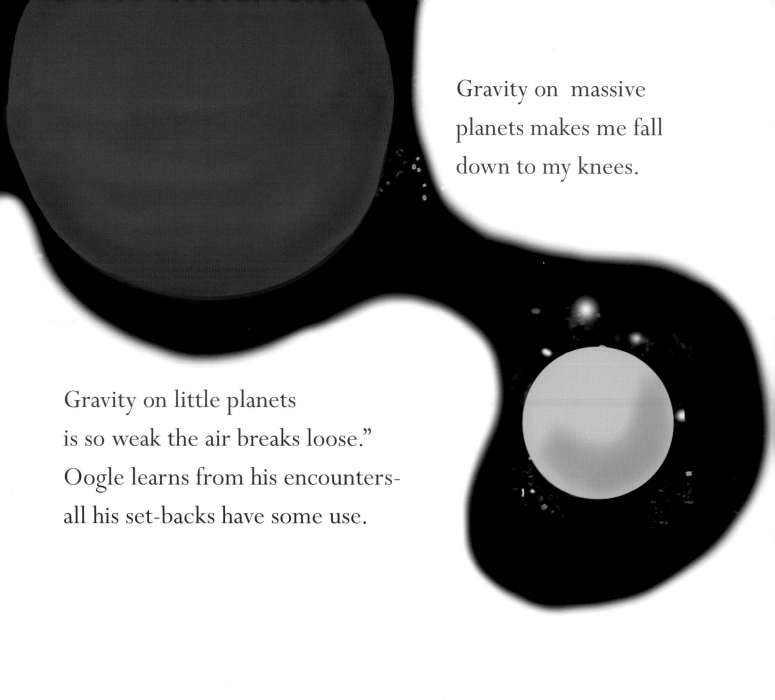

Gravity on massive
planets makes me fall
down to my knees.

Gravity on little planets
is so weak the air breaks loose."
Oogle learns from his encounters-
all his set-backs have some use.

Life needs just the right conditions.
Everything must be aligned:
gravity and air and climate.
Good planets are hard
to find!

Here's a planet with a surface,
and the gravity looks right.
It's also in a good position,
so the climate's warm and bright.

Oogle steps out of his spaceship,
takes his first sniff of the air.
"Smells like rotten eggs," thinks Oogle.
"Almost perfect. How unfair!"

Here's a planet, cloaked in water.
Oceans cover everywhere.
There's no land or even islands.
Oogle's starting to despair.

Even though the air is pleasant,
even though the climate's right,
still it's not a perfect planet.
On this one he can't alight.

"Walk on such a planet, I can't, and I don't know how to swim."

This one's much too wet for Oogle. Where's the planet right for him?

"Water-covered ocean worlds
are not the type of world for me.
Go back home again, I will.
No more planets will I see."

journey
log

ocean-covered
planet

outgoing message:
too wet it is !!

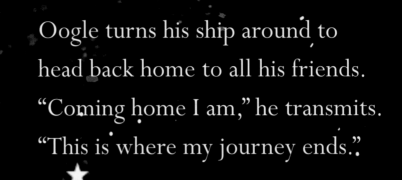

Oogle turns his ship around to
head back home to all his friends.
"Coming home I am," he transmits.
"This is where my journey ends."

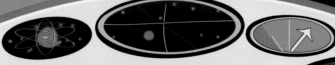

outgoing message:
coming home I am

journey
log

Then a message from the Flip-World
makes him jump up with a snap.
"Telescopes have found more stars.
Here's an update for your map."

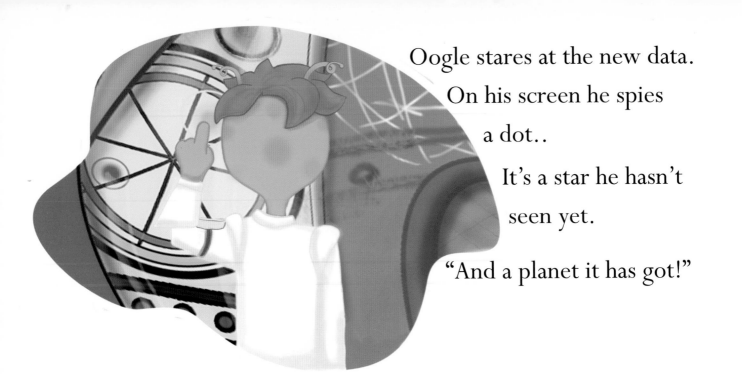

Oogle stares at the new data.
On his screen he spies
a dot..

It's a star he hasn't
seen yet.

"And a planet it has got!"

Oogle enters the position of the star into his ship.

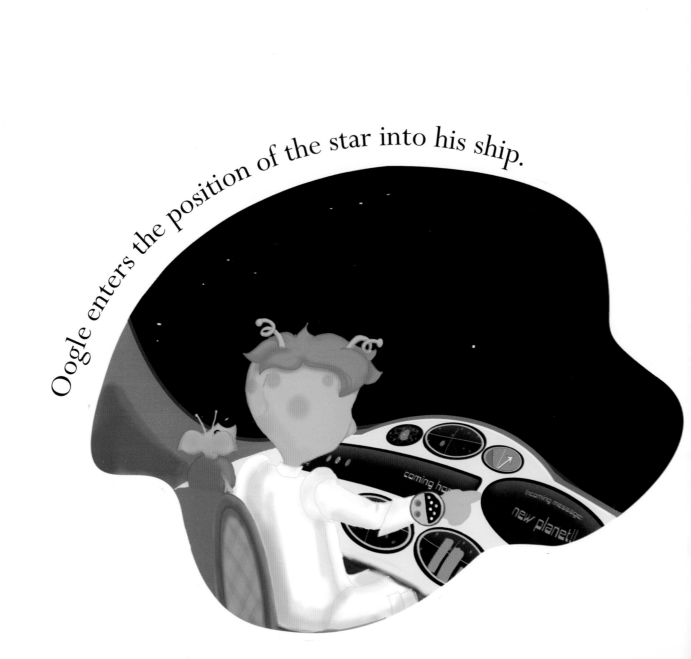

Nervously he fires the motor.

Off he goes for one last trip.

one last try

It's a planet, green and pleasant,

Circling 'round a yellow sun.

Oogle thinks, "This one looks good,

with air to breathe and room to run."

Not too hot and not too icy,

Not too big and not too small.

Could this one be right for Oogle?

Might this planet have it all?

journey
log

found one!

outgoing message:

just right it is !!

This planet is calm and peaceful.
Oogle says, "This place is great!
Big enough to keep its air, yet
small enough to shrink my weight."

"Warm enough to melt the ice, yet
cool enough the seas don't boil.
The air smells good and feels refreshing
and the ground has fertile soil."

In the distance he spies herds of brightly colored, hopping beasts.

Overhead fly flapping creatures,
"Lots of life there is, at least."

Oogle beams a hurried message back home to all his friends:
"Found a wonderful new planet. Come soon!" he recommends.

Our universe is made up of billions of stars and planets. A star is a ball of hot gas that gives off light and heat. Bigger stars tend to be hotter and brighter than smaller stars. A planet is a ball of rock or gas that circles around or orbits a star. Using powerful telescopes scientists are finding more and more extrasolar planets - planets that orbit stars other than our sun.

Our sun is a pretty average star. It has a mass of about 2 billion billion billion tons, over 300,000 times that of Earth and occupies the space of 1.3 million Earths! The surface of the sun is 5500 degrees Celsius. That's about 150 times as hot as Earth in the summertime!

Our sun has eight planets circling it. Together they make up our solar system. Four of them are rocky planets, Mercury, Venus, Earth and Mars, and four are gas planets, Jupiter, Uranus, Saturn and Neptune. The gas planets typically consist of a very tiny core of rock and ice surrounded by an enormous volume of thick swirly gases. The gas planets are hundreds of times bigger than the rocky planets. You would not be able to find a place to land on a gas planet. It would not be possible to reach all the way inside to its rocky core without being crushed by the swirling gases.

Planets, like all objects, have an invisible force called gravity that pulls other objects to them. A small planet may not have enough gravity to even hold on to air or an atmosphere. The enormous gravity of large planets would pull you so hard that you would need to use a lot of energy just to move a tiny bit. You would feel much heavier. The weaker gravity of small planets would make you feel light and allow you to jump up high without much effort.

There are no water covered planets in our solar system but scientists may have found one circling another star far away in our galaxy. So far we have not yet found another planet as suitable for life as Earth.

Space has many planets to explore and many surprises awaiting our discovery. Maybe one day you will be as brave as Oogle-Flip and set off on an exciting adventure of your own. Maybe one day you will find another planet that is right for life!

To learn more visit www.magicworldmedia.com/oogle